This Book Belongs To:

Aldrich

a gift from:

page ahead
children's literacy program

www.pageahead.org

BULLY

Jennifer Sattler

PUBLISHED BY SLEEPING BEAR PRESS

For Joan and Ryan
—JS

Bully lived in a
pond full of lilies.

And he wanted the lilies all to himself.

"Hey, you!"

shouted Bully.

"Oh, hello," said the snail.
"Have you tasted these lilies?
They're delicious!"

"Well, they're delicious and they're **MINE!**"

"Ahh, what a glorious scent,"
said a nearby dragonfly.
"It's just heavenly!"

"Hey, you!
Get out of my pond!"

"But I was just enjoying
these marvelous-smelling lilies,"
said the dragonfly.

"Their smell is the most marvelous.

Marvelous and **MINE**."

"Hey, bee!
Stop touching
those flowers!
They're **MINE!**"

"But these lilies love it
when I tickle them!"
said the bee.

"Those delicious, marvelous-smelling, tender lilies are **MINE!** Everybody, out!"

And he meant everybody.
Even the smallest fly.

Bully finally had the lilies to himself.

He made himself a crown.

He ate until his tummy ached.

He slept on a new pile of lilies every night.

Soon there was only one lily left.
"I'll keep this for myself,"
said Bully . . . to no one.

"I don't want ANYONE to smell it
or touch it
or taste it.
It's **MINE!**"

. . . So he sat on it.

The bee flew in.
"Excuse me, Bully," said the bee,
"but you're squashing that flower."

"So, what are **YOU** going to do about it?" said Bully.

The bee had an idea.

Then . . .

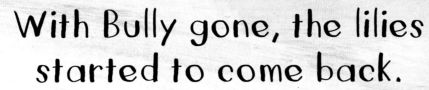

With Bully gone, the lilies
started to come back.

Bully moved on to another pond.
Only this one was mostly just . . .

mud.

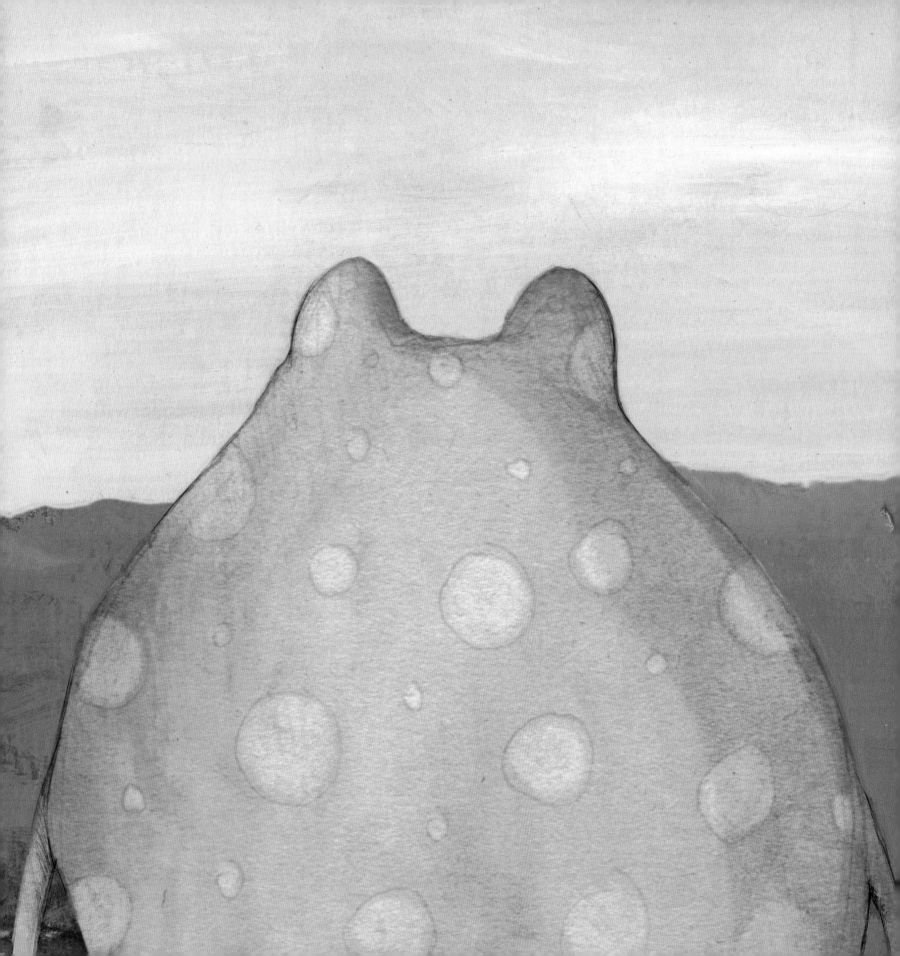

"Humph," Bully croaked. "All mine."

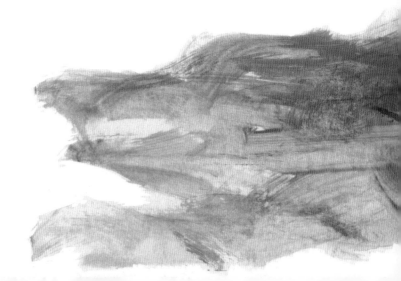

A Note about Kindness

It's easy to see that Bully is not a kind bullfrog. But what does it mean to be kind? Is it hard to do? Do you need special tools or superpowers?

Nope. Being kind is easy. If you like to draw, maybe you could draw a giant bug or a pretty flower and give it to someone who's having a hard day. You're getting bigger every day, so maybe your pants are too short. You could give them to someone who's smaller than you. Or maybe you have a toy that you haven't played with for a while? I bet there's someone little who would love to play with it. There might be a time when you see someone being unkind to another person. You could walk up to that person who was being treated poorly and say, "Hey, let's go play over there." That could be all it takes to make that person feel not so alone and to remind them that although there are bullies out there, there are a lot more kind people. And you're one of them.

Try this next time you're out with your mom or dad or your favorite grown-up: smile at everyone you see. You'll start to see faces smiling back at you, like flowers bursting open! Who knows? It might be like being in a whole pond full of lilies!

—Jennifer